Puffin Books
Editor: Kaye Webb

Joe and Timothy Together

Joe and Timothy lived in the same house. They
weren't brothers, just very good friends, and they
didn't even live very close, because Joe's family were
right at the top of their tall house, and Timothy lived
at the very bottom, in the basement, where he could
only see people's legs going by if they went out to
the shops.

All sorts of other people lived in the house too, which
made it rather a special, exciting place to explore.
There was kind, rosy Mr Christopherson, who had
once been a famous clown, and old Mrs Lemon, who
took them to the launderette, and of course their
friend Jessie, the little girl who lived somewhere in
the middle, neither up nor down.

Yes, the tall house really was a good place to live. You'd
never find a better spot than the flat roof for watching
rockets and bonfires on Guy Fawkes' night, or meet
such a lot of very kind friends anywhere else to help
celebrate a very special birthday.

Dorothy Edwards is one of the favourite Puffin authors.
Besides having written another book of stories about
lively, enthusiastic young Joe and Timothy (*Tales of
Joe and Timothy*) she is the creator of the classic series,
My Naughty Little Sister, *My Naughty Little Sister's
Friends* and *When My Naughty Little Sister Was
Good*, which have all appeared in Young Puffins.

Dorothy Edwards

Joe and Timothy Together

Illustrated by Reintje Venema

Puffin Books

Puffin Books,
Penguin Books Ltd,
Harmondsworth, Middlesex, England
Penguin Books Australia Ltd,
Ringwood, Victoria, Australia
Penguin Books Canada Ltd,
41 Steelcase Road West, Markham, Ontario, Canada
Penguin Books (N.Z.) Ltd,
182–190 Wairau Road, Auckland 10, New Zealand

First published by Methuen Children's Books Ltd 1971
Published in Puffin Books 1975

Made and printed in Great Britain by
Cox & Wyman Ltd, London, Reading and Fakenham
Set in Monotype Bembo

To Mark Alan Francis Brunt
my Birthday Boy, with love

Contents

Mr Lemon's notion

If you ever fly up in the air in a helicopter, you might look down, down and see away below among the green fields and hills a big straggly town with a river running through it, and trains rushing towards it, and a park like a green carpet trimmed with coloured flower-beds, and factories with big chimneys and streets and streets of houses of all sizes, small ones with back gardens and very, very tall ones.

You might even fly over a very tall house with a flat rooftop that has a line of washing flapping on it, and a far-off yard below where there are two lines of washing, and you never know, that might be the very tall house in the very smoky town where Joe and his friends Timothy and Jessie are living! If it is, you will know that the washing on the rooftop was done by Joe's Mum who lives up there, and the washing down below was done by Timothy's mother who puts out two lines every day now that she has the little baby girl Dawn Gloria to wash for as well as Timothy and his Dad.

Joe and Timothy's mothers are lucky because if they want to they can do their washing at home and put it out to dry in the open air, but the other ladies in the tall house take their washing to the launderette and bring it home again, dry enough to iron.

There hasn't always been a launderette in the Big Town, and before it opened the ladies who lived in Joe's and Timothy's house had had to dry their washing indoors, or else put it out of the window on poles; so, although the launderette is quite a long way away on the other side of the Park, they think it is well worth the walk. At least most of them do. There are people like Mrs Lemon whose legs are sometimes bad and who can't carry heavy washing through the streets, who wish they had Joe's Mum's roof space and Timothy's Mum's yard to do their drying in.

Of course, the ladies who go to the launderette are very kind and they often take the washing for those who can't get there.

Joe's Mum always took Mrs Lemon's washing for her and Joe and Timothy and Jessie often went with her.

Mrs Lemon was very interested to hear about the launderette, because when she was young she used to work in a laundry, ironing clothes, and she just couldn't believe all the things Joe and Timothy told her about it.

'It's a very big place,' said Joe, 'with lots and lots of washing machines doing lots and lots of washing.'

'They all go, bubble bubble, swish-swosh,' said Jessie, the little brown girl.

'And there's drying machines, and dry-cleaning machines,' said Timothy.

Mrs Lemon said, 'It's a marvel how they think up these ideas. A washing shop! My, my!'

'And there's three ironing machines too,' said Joe's Mum. 'If I hadn't got my washing-machine at home, I'd feel like going there just to iron my sheets on those machines.'

And Mrs Lemon said, 'My, my!' again. 'Ironing machines. Well, I never did . . .'

So, one day, when Mrs Lemon's boy Terry came to visit her with his car, and asked her if she'd like to go out for a ride it was hardly surprising really that she should say, 'Well now, Terry, I tell you where I would like to go. I'd like to go over to the other side of the Town and take a look at that launderette there.'

Terry was very surprised, because he thought his Mum would have liked a run out to the country, but she said, 'No. I just want to see it for myself, and, as young Joe and Timothy and Jessie have told me so much about it, let's take them too, so they can point things out to me.'

And she said, while she was about it, she might as well take some sheets and things with her, to try out the machines!

Of course, the three little friends were very pleased to

go with Mrs Lemon in her Terry's car to the launderette. When they got there, Mrs Lemon said, 'Now, Terry, you just bring in my bundle and put it by that empty machine over there and then you can go. Call back for me at four o'clock.' She said, 'I think I'm going to enjoy myself!'

And do you know, Mrs Lemon enjoyed herself very much, and so did Joe and Timothy and Jessie – they enjoyed themselves too. Going to the launderette with Mrs

Lemon was like a holiday, because she was so pleased and excited about everything. It wasn't like an ordinary visit at all.

There are machines in the launderette where you can

get things to drink like tea and coffee and orange-squash, and things to eat such as sandwiches, buns and biscuits.

After Joe had shown Mrs Lemon how to put the clothes into the machine, and Jessie had shown her where to get the washing-powder and Timothy had explained about putting the money in, and the washing had started to swish about, Mrs Lemon said, 'Now for a nice cup of tea!'

She bought some orange-squash and biscuits for the children and they sat in a row eating and drinking and watching Mrs Lemon's washing going round and round.

It was great fun because Mrs Lemon said, 'Look! there's Dad's shirt!' and 'Look, there's my blue apron!' and 'There now! That's the pillow-case with the darn in it – see the darn?' and she made such a game of it that the children were soon shouting and pointing and jumping up and down, and if they hadn't drunk their orange-squash first they would probably have spilled it all over the floor.

People kept coming in and out of the launderette, and soon Mrs Lemon was waving to some old friends who came and talked to her and smiled at Joe and Timothy and Jessie when Mrs Lemon said, 'These are my neighbours' kiddies – come to help me with the wash!'

When Mrs Lemon's things were washed and dried and she had put her sheets and a table-cloth through the ironing machine there was still some time left before four o'clock when her Terry was to come to fetch them, so she helped an old lady who was trying to put some things into a washing machine and explained all about it to her, just as if she had been doing it herself for ages!

When Terry came Mrs Lemon was really sorry to go home and when she did get back she did nothing but talk and talk about the wonderful launderette and how much nicer it was than the laundry where she had worked when she was young and what a treat it was to see washing doing itself.

Mr Lemon told Jessie's Mum that he didn't think Mrs Lemon had enjoyed herself so much for years. He said it had been as good as a trip to the seaside to her.

Jessie's Mum had been very surprised, she said: 'I can't say I like going to the launderette very much – it takes up so much time. It's a pity Mrs Lemon can't manage the journey – I'm sure some of us would be only too glad to let her take and do our washing for us.'

Of course Jessie's mother was only joking. But that was when Mr Lemon first started having his Notion.

First of all he talked to his mate, Nobby, about it. Then he talked to Jessie's Mum and one or two of the other tall house ladies and at last he said to Mrs Lemon:

'How would you like to take a trip to the launderette once a week and make a day of it?'

Mrs Lemon stared at him.

Mr Lemon said, 'I've talked to young Nobby and some

of the neighbours and the upshot's this: the ladies would be obliged if you could see to their washing for them, and young Nobby can run you and their bundles over to that launderette in his van one morning a week and pick you up again at the end of the day. The neighbours will all give you something for your trouble so you'll be able to earn yourself some pin-money and you'll meet some of your old friends and have a good time. What do you say?'

So that's what happens now. Once a week Mrs Lemon goes off in Nobby's van with the washing from the tall house. She looks forward to it very much. She meets lots of her old friends and has made many new ones and everyone is very happy.

Joe, Timothy and Jessie are happy, too, because Mrs Lemon often takes them with her and she always says, 'If it hadn't been for those children telling me about the launderette, I'd never have wanted to see it, and if I hadn't seen it, Mr Lemon would never have had that Notion of his.'

Timothy makes friends with a clown

I wonder if you like clowns?

Joe and Timothy and Jessie like them very much, though there *was* a time when Timothy didn't like them at all. If there were any clowns walking about the High Street collecting money for Oxfam or advertising the circus, Joe and Jessie would laugh and push forward to see them, but Timothy would go behind his mother and not look.

Once a clown was in the Supermarket giving away balloons and Timothy wouldn't even take a red balloon from him, though he loves red balloons!

He was just frightened of clowns' funny painted faces. He couldn't help it. *He just didn't like clowns.*

Timothy's mother was quite worried about this, and she spoke about it to the Special Lady who comes to the Park to play games with the children who aren't old enough to go to school.

The Special Lady said, 'Don't worry, he'll get over it.
When I was a little girl I couldn't bear Vicars. I just
couldn't bear those black fronts and the white back-to-
front collars. It used to make me cry to see them. I would
never go to Sunday School treats! But I got over it in
time.'

So Timothy's Mum said, 'Well, I'll just have to have patience.'

Now, as you know, Timothy's family live right at the bottom of the tall, tall house. He sleeps in a little bedroom with his baby sister, Dawn Gloria. Sometimes, when he is in bed at night he hears noises over his head.

They aren't loud noises – just little scratching sounds like someone moving a chair or tiny soft pat-pat noises like some quiet person walking about.

Timothy doesn't mind these noises because he knows the people who are making them. He knows it is old Mr and Mrs Christopherson who live just above his home. They are very quiet old people and Timothy only hears them at night. During the day his Mum mostly has the radio on all the time, and in the evening his Dad likes to look at the telly so things aren't usually quiet enough for anyone to hear the Christophersons.

Old Mr Christopherson is a dear old rosy man. Timothy often sees his nice old trotty legs going past the window when he looks up from whatever he is doing in his downstairs home. Mr Christopherson goes off to do the shopping every day because Mrs Christopherson can't get about now. Sometimes when the weather is wet Joe's Mum pops down to see what he wants from the shops and goes and gets it for him.

Timothy is always pleased when he sees Mr Christopherson's legs going by, because one day, when Timothy

18

happened to be standing on a chair near the window, the legs had stopped, and Mr Christopherson had bent down and looked at Timothy and pulled a funny face at him, which had made Timothy laugh every time he thought about it afterwards.

Well now, one day when Joe had gone out for a ride on Mr Lemon's lorry to see his country Gran, and Jessie had gone out with her Mum and some of her brothers and sisters to have tea with one of her aunties, Timothy didn't know what to do with himself.

It had been all right while Dawn Gloria was awake; he could play games to make her laugh, but during the afternoon she liked to go to sleep for a while, and although Timothy tried to keep her awake by playing 'peep-bo' behind the curtain, and although she thought that a lovely game, all the same she went right off to sleep in the middle of a smile, and left Timothy to amuse himself.

And Timothy amused himself by going out through the door at the back of his mother's bedroom that led into the house, and setting off upstairs as he had done on the day when he first met Joe.

This time he played a pretending game that they some-times played at the Special Lady's meetings, but he played it going upstairs, not just walking round.

He sang, 'One, two, buckle my shoe,' as he went up two stairs, and then he stopped and pretended to fasten his shoe.

Then he sang, 'Three, four, knock at the door,' and went up two more stairs, and knocked on the next stair with his hand.

'Five, six, pick up sticks,' he sang as he went up two more stairs, and he pretended to pick up some sticks.

And he had just finished singing, 'Seven, eight, lay them straight,' and pretended to lay them straight in the funny way that used to make the Special Lady and all the children laugh, when he looked up and saw old Mr Christopherson standing outside his door, looking down, and Mr Christopherson was laughing.

'Eleven, twelve, dig and delve,' sang Timothy, and did some funny pretending digging, lifting his pretending spade and acting that it was funny hard work.

And then Timothy just had to stop digging and delving and laugh himself, because there was old Mr Christopherson pretending that *he* was digging and delving too, and he was being *so* funny, pretending that his spade was stuck, and then pretending that he pulled it so hard he hit himself on the nose with it, that Timothy could hardly believe he hadn't got a real spade there.

When Timothy had stopped laughing, Mr Christopherson said, 'On your own today then, laddie?' and Timothy said, 'Yes.'

He told the nice old man that his friends were out and that Dawn Gloria was asleep, and that he was just going for a walk in the house for something to do.

'Well now,' said Mr Christopherson, 'how would you like to come and say hello to my Daisy? She's feeling very much perkier today and I know she'd like a visitor.'

Mr Christopherson called Mrs Christopherson his Daisy. Timothy had never been to visit her before, although sometimes he had noticed her peeping out of the window when his Mum took him out. She had looked such a friendly old lady, and once she had waved to Dawn Gloria and Dawn Gloria had waved back. Timothy thought it would be very nice to go and see her.

Old Mrs Christopherson was a very tiny, thin old lady. She sat in a big chair by the window with lots of cushions and pillows behind her back, and a big fat cushion under her feet. Timothy thought she was very, very old.

She was very pleased to see Timothy. She said, 'You are the little boy from underneath. I am glad you've come to see me. I often hear you playing with your baby sister. She's got such a pretty laugh, bless her heart.'

Timothy was surprised to hear that the old lady listened to him playing with Dawn Gloria. He said, 'Do you hear when I get cross and shout?' and the old lady said she did. Then she said, 'Give the laddie a sweetie, Dobby,' and Mr Christopherson got a blue and red tin down from a shelf and held it out to Timothy. 'Take two,' he said, and Timothy took two toffees and Mr Christopherson took two as well.

Timothy looked all round the room where Mrs
Christopherson was sitting. He specially looked at a big
picture on the wall by her chair. It was a picture of a pretty
lady in a frilly short dress standing up on the back of a
horse that was running along underneath a round paper
hoop. The lady was just going to jump through the hoop.
There was lots of writing under the picture of the lady,

but Timothy doesn't read yet, so he didn't know what it said.

'That's a nice picture,' said Timothy.

'That's Daisy herself,' said the rosy old man. 'That's Mrs Christopherson when she was Queen of the Ring!'

Timothy was very surprised, and he looked hard at the old lady in the chair. 'And she might be at it now if it wasn't for her falling off and upsetting her back,' said Mr Christopherson. And then, because he saw Timothy was really interested in Mrs Christopherson's Queen of the Ring picture, he took a book out of the drawer and opened it, and soon he was showing Timothy lots of pictures. They were old-looking pictures of a very pretty young lady in all sorts of frilly and sparkling dresses. Sometimes she was riding on a horse, sometimes she was standing by one, and there was a picture of two men riding on horses and the young lady was standing high up with her feet on the shoulders of the two young men.

'That's Daisy and her brothers,' said Mr Christopherson.

And then – he turned over a page, and, oh dear! There was a picture of a clown! Mr Christopherson turned over and there were more clown-pictures. There was a dancing clown in a top-hat, a clown pretending to play tunes on a tennis-racquet, a clown with striped trousers standing on his head. Clowns!

'What's the matter, laddie?' said Mr Christopherson.

'They're *clowns*,' said Timothy.

'They're ME,' said the nice rosy old man. 'They are all pictures of me.'

'Dobby is a very famous clown,' said the tiny old lady. 'My Dobby is the funniest clown in the world.'

Timothy couldn't believe it.

'But you don't look like *that*,' he said. 'Your face is *ordinary*.'

And Mr Christopherson laughed. 'This is my real face,' he said. 'The funny face is just painted on. I've got some special stuff I paint my face with. Sometimes I make it look happy – ' and he smiled – 'and sometimes I make it look miserable' – and he pulled a miserable face. 'It's hard work painting your face properly, I can tell you.'

'Oh,' said Timothy, 'I didn't know clowns had ordinary faces underneath.'

'Of course they have,' said Mr Christopherson.

'Ah, but it's not the face that makes the clown,' said the old lady. 'It's the funny things they do to make people laugh.'

'Like you did just now – digging and delving?' asked Timothy.

'That's right,' said the nice old clown. 'And you did a real comic piece of digging yourself, laddie. In fact, it was really funny. It was really funny, Daisy,' he said to the old lady. 'Who knows, one day he may be a clown himself?'

'He can make his baby sister laugh now,' said the dear old thin lady.

And before Timothy left to go downstairs, Mr Christopherson gave him a new stick of white face-paint to put away in case he ever decided to become a clown.

And that is why Joe and Jessie *and* Timothy now like clowns.

Jessie's big brothers

Jessie who lives in the middle of the tall house has some older brothers and sisters. Some of them aren't living at home any more. Jessie's big sister, Margaret, is a nurse in a hospital, and her big brothers, Cyril and George, live in a house in another street because there is no room for them in the home in the tall house.

Every day Jessie's mother goes round to the room where Cyril and George live and tidies it up for them. Jessie's Mum is a very fussy lady, she likes everything to be neat, and as Cyril and George are untidy boys there is always plenty for her to do in that room.

Sometimes Jessie stays to play with Joe and Timothy while her mother goes round to the boys' room, but sometimes she goes too, and while her Mum makes the boys' beds and shakes out their mats, Jessie tidies up the books and records and papers that are lying about everywhere, and dusts the table.

Jessie is fussy too, and soon she and her mother make the room look beautifully tidy again.

One day Joe and Timothy were playing on the landing outside Jessie's home. There is plenty of room there and the big window gives them lots of light to see by. They were playing with their cars as usual when Jessie came out of her door and spoke to them. Jessie had been playing hospitals with her dolly and she was wearing a cap and apron with red crosses on them.

Jessie said, 'My Mum says you must be careful to pick up all those cars when you've finished playing with them, because someone might tread on one and have a bad accident on the stairs.'

Timothy said he knew that, because his Mum had told him already, and Joe said, yes he knew that too! He said he had five cars and Timothy had seven cars and they always count them when they pick them up to make sure there are none left lying about.

Jessie said, 'Well, if you'd like to pick them up now my mother says you can come to the Park with us. Go and ask your Mums if you can come.'

Joe's Mum and Timothy's Mum both said it was very kind of Jessie's mother because it wasn't her turn to take the children today, but Jessie's mother said, 'Well, I have to call in to the boys' place on the way to see their land-lady about the washing. She wasn't in there this morning when I went to clean up. It's on the way to the Park. It seems a pity not to do the two things at the same time.'

So off they went.

Joe and Timothy knew Cyril and George quite well, but they had never been to their room before. When they got to the house Jessie's Mum said, 'Here, Jessie, take the key and go up to the boys' room with Joe and Timothy while I speak to Mrs Eaves' – Mrs Eaves was the boys' landlady.

It was a very interesting room, right at the top of Mrs Eaves's house. Jessie's brother Cyril works on the railway. He looks after the engines at the moment but very soon he will be able to drive them. Mrs Eaves's old Dad who lives with her used to be a railwayman and he has given Cyril an old oil-lamp off a steam train and an old-fashioned porter's hat. Cyril keeps them on a shelf over his bed.

George is still at school and he wants to work on a farm one day. He has lots of books about farming and he has stuck pictures of cows and pigs and tractors on the wall by *his* bed. George is very clever and Jessie told Joe and Timothy that later on he is going to a college where he can learn about farming.

Jessie said, 'My Dadda says he doesn't know where George gets the idea from, because no one in our family ever wanted to be a farmer before.'

George and Cyril have a big record-player and a lot of records in a rack. Cyril has painted the rack orange and blue, and George has written a list of all the records in blue and orange writing and hung it on the wall over the record-player.

There is a funny old gramophone in the corner of the boys' room. It has a big green horn and there are lots of records with pictures of little white dogs listening to a gramophone with a horn on them.

'That one belongs to Mrs Eaves's old Dad,' Jessie said. 'He comes up here when he wants some music because Mrs Eaves doesn't like him playing it downstairs. She can't hear her TV if he does.'

Just then Jessie's mother came to take them to the Park and all the way there the three friends talked about the things in George's and Cyril's room.

Joe said, 'I'd like a record-player. If I had a record-player I'd never stop playing it.'

Timothy said, 'I think I'd like a gramophone with a horn like Mrs Eaves's Dad's. You only switch the record-player on, but you have to wind the gramophone up before it will play.'

It wasn't the Special Lady's day that day, but when they arrived at the playground they found her there anyway. She was sitting on the seat by the swings and she had a jumper on that was as yellow as Jessie's hair-ribbons. She smiled when she saw the children and said, 'Snap! Your ribbons – my jumper!' to Jessie.

'What are you here for, Special Lady?' Jessie said. 'This isn't your day.'

'Are you going to play with us?' asked Timothy. 'I do hope so.'

But the Special Lady laughed and said, 'Oh no! I've just come down to talk to the man who mends the swings. I tied some up the other day because they didn't look safe to me and he's meeting me here to talk about them. He should have been here ten minutes ago. I don't know what's keeping him.'

'Never mind,' said Jessie. 'We will stay and keep you company if you like,' and the Special Lady said that was just what she wanted – some company to help her while away the time, and she asked the children what they had been doing.

So then it was Joe's and Timothy's turn to talk and they told her all about the visit to the boys' room. About the record-player and the gramophone and George's farm pictures and the old railway-porter's hat

'And George has lots of books about farms,' said Joe.

'My boy George thinks of nothing but farms,' said Jessie's mother, and she told the Special Lady all the things about George that Jessie had told Joe and Timothy. 'To hear him talk you would think he knows everything in the world about farms,' she said. 'Only he hasn't even visited one yet.'

The Special Lady listened very hard and then she said, 'Now *that* gives me an idea!' But she didn't say any more then because she saw the swing-mender man hurrying down the path towards her.

But a few days afterwards Jessie knew all about the Special Lady's idea and it wasn't long before Joe and Timothy knew too.

The Special Lady's idea had been this: she had an uncle who looked after a big farm where there were lots of cows and sheep. She had gone home at once after she had finished talking to the swing-mender man and had written a letter to her uncle telling him all about George, and her uncle had written back to say he would be glad if George could come and spend the summer holidays on his farm and help the farm-workers and get an idea of how farms really worked.

Jessie said, 'That George is so pleased! He smiled so much his ears nearly met at the back of his neck!'

And Joe and Timothy laughed so much when she said that it's a wonder their ears didn't meet round at the back of their necks too!

Miss Smithers's window

When Joe's mother wants to hang her washing out she climbs out of her kitchen window and pegs it to the clothes line on the flat roof outside, where Joe's Dad grows tomatoes in a greenhouse and Joe and Timothy sometimes play.

There is a wall all round the roof so you can't fall off, and quite near Joe's Dad's greenhouse there is a thing like a wooden box with a glass lid which is a window in the ceiling of the room that is underneath that bit of roof. You can't look down into that room, though, because the lady called Miss Smithers who lives there has fastened a lacy net curtain across it; and you can't drop things on it by accident and break the glass because Joe's Dad has made a wire-netting cover to fit over the top.

Joe and Timothy can't see Miss Smithers, but they do know when she is at home because they can hear her wireless, and sometimes they hear her kettle which whistles when it begins to boil.

Joe's Mum doesn't like them to listen by Miss Smithers's window. She says it is rude to listen to other people, but as that rooftop is rather small and fairly quiet, you can't help hearing sometimes, even if you don't mean to.

One warm summer morning Joe and Timothy were playing out on the rooftop with their toy cars and some toy traffic-lights that Timothy's Auntie Dolly had sent him. It was so warm they had only got their woolly

shorts on, and they were playing in the shady part near Joe's Mum's kitchen window, because the sunny part of the roof was already getting too warm to kneel on.

They were having a lovely game. Joe had borrowed his Mum's pepper-pot from the kitchen window-sill and they were pretending that it was a policeman. Joe made a cross, shouting policeman's voice, and Timothy made a gruff, grown-up driver's voice and they pretended to have quarrels about the traffic.

'I'm not going to take any notice of those old traffic-lights,' said gruff grown-up-voiced Timothy, and he pushed a yellow lorry straight across the crossing – even though the lights were red which means STOP.

'Stop at once!' cried the cross-shouting policeman Joe. 'Stop, or I'll send you to prison!' and he bumped his Mum's pepper-pot up and down.

'I don't care,' said gruff Timothy. 'You can't catch me, mate!' And he pushed the yellow lorry so hard it went right across the roof, out of the shadow, into the sunshine, and then into the shadow of Miss Smithers's window where it crashed against the wooden side, turned over on to its back and lay with its wheels spinning round and round.

Joe got up. 'Now you've had a terrible accident, you silly man,' he shouted, and he carried the pepper-pot policeman across the warm roof to where the lorry was lying. 'You must come to the police station,' he said in his

35

cross-shouting voice, and he bent down and picked the lorry up.

And as he bent down, a crosser and a shoutinger voice called out from behind him, 'Oh, shut up! Shut up and GO AWAY!'

Poor Joe! He *was* startled. He had never heard a cackly, crackly, screechy voice like that before!

'Go away! Go away! Go away!' it shouted.

And Joe *did* go away. He dropped the yellow lorry, and he ran back to Timothy, who was kneeling up very straight with his mouth saying 'O'.

'I didn't do anything,' said Joe. 'I didn't do *anything* and it *shouted*!' Joe's face had gone very red and if he hadn't been a big boy he might have cried.

'I know, wasn't it *awful*?' whispered Timothy. 'Was it Miss Smithers?'

'I don't think so,' Joe whispered back. 'It doesn't sound like her. I think Miss Smithers has gone to work. My Mum says when there's no wireless on it means she's out.'

'Are you going to tell your Mum?' said Timothy in a low voice.

But Joe said, 'No, she might be cross and say I must have been naughty.'

So the two little boys sat very quiet on the warm roof-top for a while, listening; but nothing happened. Then Timothy said, 'Joe', and Joe whispered, 'Yes?'

And Timothy said, 'Joe, I'm going to get that lorry!'

And Timothy got up, walked out into the sunshine right across to Miss Smithers's window and picked the yellow lorry up again.

And nothing happened.

There wasn't a sound. No screechy cackly voice – nothing! It was very still and quiet, and the sunshine was now very hot.

Joe walked over to where Timothy was standing and they both listened hard. Perhaps they hadn't really heard anything at all? Perhaps it had been a sort of pretending? Like Joe pretending to be a grown-up lorry driver.

'It wasn't anyone,' said Joe, and he just gave two little kicks against the wooden side of Miss Smithers's window to show he wasn't afraid any more. Kick, kick.

'Come in! Don't knock! Come in,' called the screechy, cackly voice.

'Ring the bell, knock the knocker,
Peep through the keyhole.
Lift up the latch, wipe your boots,
And WALK IN'

it said. Joe looked at Timothy, Timothy looked at Joe.

'It wants us to go in!' said Joe. 'But we can't, the window's shut. Anyway, I don't want to.'

'Walk in, walk in,' said the voice. It wasn't cross now – only screechy. 'Wipe your boots,' it said. 'Wipe your boots.'

'I don't like it,' said Timothy. 'I think I want to go home, Joe!'

'OH! GO AWAY! GO AWAY!' The voice was very cross again, so the little boys ran across the roof and climbed through the kitchen window and ran to Joe's Mum who was polishing the brass in the living-room.

When he saw his Mum's nice kind face Joe forgot all about not telling her about that strange voice, he began to tell her straight away, and every time he stopped, Timothy said something

'From Miss Smithers's window. He *shouted* at me. He said "GO AWAY!"'

'Joe wasn't being naughty, even!'

'He said, "Ring the bell, knock the knocker."'

'I didn't like him. He was *nasty*!'

'My goodness me!' said Joe's mother when they stopped at last. 'You must have heard old Sam! He's Miss Smithers's old grandad's parrot. *Surely* you boys weren't afraid of old Sam?'

Joe and Timothy peeped at each other. Had they been frightened? Surely not.

Joe's mother said that every summer when Miss Smithers's old grandad went to the seaside with the Old Folks, Miss Smithers minded Sam for him.

She told them that Sam was a big grey bird who lived in a cage and that Miss Smithers's old grandad had had him for years and had taught him to talk. Sam could say

lots of little rhymes, and he could sing too, but he had also
learned to copy the things he heard the old grandad say.
'Miss Smithers says he sounds just like her grandad sometimes – especially when he shouts,' Joe's Mum said.

Joe said, 'Well, he sounds very cross.' And his Mum
said, 'Well that poor old man has a bad leg so he can't
get out very much. I expect he is cross sometimes. But he's
never cross with Sam. Miss Smithers says Sam is the apple
of his eye!'

It was soon time for Timothy to go downstairs for his
dinner and Joe went part of the way with him. On their
way down they met Jessie who had just come back from
the swimming-baths with one of her sisters, and her hair
was all wet.

Timothy began to tell Jessie all about Sam the parrot.
But Jessie said, 'I know all about that bad old bird!
Doesn't he shout sometimes!'

Jessie said, 'Have you heard him say:

"Ring the bell, knock the knocker,
Peep through the keyhole.
Lift up the latch, wipe your boots,
And WALK IN"?'

And as Jessie said 'Ring the bell' she pulled one of her
little wet curls. When she said 'Knock the knocker' she
tapped her forehead. When she said 'Peep through the

keyhole' she made an 'O' with her thumb and finger and peeped through it with one of her bright little eyes.

When she said 'Lift up the latch' she put her finger under her nose and lifted it up. When she said 'Wipe your boots' she rubbed her finger on her chin, and when she said 'Walk in' she opened her mouth and popped her finger inside.

Joe and Timothy stared.

'The Special Lady taught us to play that game once when you weren't there,' Jessie said. 'I'll show you how to play it sometime. It's a funny game when you do it quickly.'

Joe said, 'I wonder how Miss Smithers's grandad came to know that game?'

'I expect he played it when he was a little boy,' clever Jessie said.

Nights and O.T.

One day, Timothy who lives right at the bottom of the tall, tall house, went upstairs to see if his friend, Joe, who lives right up at the very top, wanted to play.

When Timothy got to the landing where Jessie their little friend lived, he found her standing outside her door, and he asked her to come too.

'Come on, Jessie,' Timothy said. He stretched out his arms and made aeroplane noises all down the landing and up the stairs and Jessie went behind him making aeroplane noises too.

Now there is a very nice lady called Mrs Lambert who lives just under Joe's home. She has a big, grown-up son called Arnie who lives with her. Joe and Timothy like Arnie because he always talks to them when he sees them, even though he is quite old – and because once when he was tidying his bedroom, he gave them a model battleship each that he had made himself.

On this day, when Timothy and the little brown girl Jessie went up to call for Joe, they were very surprised

because when they came to Mrs Lambert's landing she opened her door and said, 'Sh! Sh! Go quietly, please, children. My Arnie's ON NIGHTS!'

They didn't know what she meant, but she held her finger to her lips and looked so quiet, that Timothy and Jessie just nodded their heads and crept upstairs to Joe's home without making any more noise at all.

When they arrived at Joe's home among the chimney-pots they found his door open, and, as they peeped in, Joe's Mum looked out and said, 'Come in, Timothy and Jessie but *please* take your shoes off! Arnie Lambert is on nights and the least sound wakes him up!'

So Jessie and Timothy took their shoes off, and crept down the shiny lino behind Joe's mother to the room where Joe was sitting at the table playing with his farm-yard animals.

Jessie whispered, 'Hello,' to Joe, but Joe said, 'You don't have to whisper Jessie. It's only *feet*. Mrs Lambert says *she* likes to hear them. She says she likes to think she's got friends above – but they upset Arnie when he's on nights.'

Timothy did wish he knew what 'on nights' meant, but he didn't like to ask, because everyone talked as if he ought to know, so he was glad when Jessie said, 'What does this "on nights" mean?'

Joe said he didn't know, and Timothy was glad then and said *he* didn't know either.

'I'll ask your Mum, Joe,' Jessie said. So Jessie asked Joe's mother, and she told the children that Arnie was working all night in the factory instead of in the daytime. She said he was doing shifts – which meant he wouldn't always work all night – only sometimes.

'When Arnie is on nights, he will be sleeping in the daytime, and we shall have to be very careful not to wake him up,' she said.

Joe's Mum said it was a good thing for Mrs Lambert when Arnie was on nights because he earned more money when he did this, and he was saving all his extra money to take Mrs Lambert away for a holiday over the sea to a place called Ostend.

'Mrs Lambert could do with a change,' said Joe's kind Mum, 'so we must make it easy for Arnie. It's a bit of a nuisance though, because this lino makes a dreadful clatter when anything is dropped on it.'

So after that, when the children played in Joe's home and Arnie Lambert was on nights it was quite an adventure, and they made up quiet, giggly games when they crept about.

But then something happened that Joe didn't like much. His Daddy began to come in from work long after Joe was in bed and asleep.

Joe's Dad works out of doors. He helps to make the big holes in the road and lay pipes in them, and one of the nice things for Joe has been to watch for him every night from the window of Jessie's landing, and when he sees him coming to run down the stairs of the big house to meet him.

When they meet, his Dad picks him up, and swings him high in the air before they go upstairs together. His mother gets Joe ready for bed while his father eats his supper, and his Dad always leaves a little bit of his pudding in the dish for Joe.

His Mum would say, 'Oh dear, Joe's already had his supper and cleaned his teeth!'

And his Dad would say, 'Well, a morsel more won't hurt him, and he can clean his teeth again! He'll need a lot of your good cooking if he's going to be a strong Roadie like me!'

And he would bend his arm until it was all lumpy to show how strong he was, and Joe would feel the lumps to see how hard they were. And they would all laugh together.

And then he stopped coming home at his usual time.

The first night his Mum said, 'Daddy will be late tonight; he is doing O.T. for a week or so. They have a rush job on. They have to get all the holes in the road filled in by the time the Queen comes to open the New Bridge.'

Joe's Mum told him that O.T. was a way of saying 'overtime'. She said that if his Dad worked more hours than usual in any day it was called O.T. And he got lots more money for working overtime.

'Just like Arnie Lambert on nights,' Joe said.

Next day, Joe told Timothy and Jessie that his Dad was working O.T. He was quite surprised when nobody asked him what it meant. Instead, Timothy just said, 'My Dad does O.T. sometimes, and sometimes he has to work on Sunday when they want the buildings put up more quickly.'

And Jessie said, 'My Dadda does lots of O.T. on the buses and he works lots of Sundays!'

And after that they often talked about O.T. and working on nights.

Well now, one day when Jessie and Timothy went up to call for their friend Joe they had a great surprise. Joe opened the door to them, and the first thing Joe said was, 'You won't have to take your shoes off any more.'

And there, all over the floor, was a lovely soft new carpet – in the passage and all over the room where the children usually played. It was a beautiful greeny goldy carpet and it covered all the floor right up.

'It's lovely to roll on,' Joe said, and he lay on the floor to show how lovely it was.

So of course Timothy and Jessie rolled on it too. It certainly was nice – so thick and soft and springy! And it was beautifully quiet for walking on.

Joe's mother said, 'Joe's Daddy bought it with the money he got for doing O.T. He isn't doing O.T. any more, but now we can walk about without waking poor Arnie up, and without having to remember to creep!'

'And Arnie can make a lot of money on nights and take Mrs Lambert to Ostend,' said Jessie.

But Joe said, 'It's nice to have the carpet, but I am glad my Dad will be coming home early again.'

The Special Offer pens

All the ladies who live in the tall, tall house in the big town like Special Offers. If a thing in a shop is called a Special Offer they always buy it, and if something in the paper is called a Special Offer and one of the ladies sends for it, all the other ladies send for it too, as soon as they have seen what it looks like.

So one day when the milkman who serves all the people in the tall house came along with a Special Offer of coloured pens, all the tall house ladies decided to have extra milk for a time so they could have the Special Offer pens.

Timothy's Mum got her pens first because of course they always need extra milk for the baby and for Timothy's Dad who likes it for his supper. But it wasn't long before Joe's and Jessie's mothers got their pens too, and of course as Joe's and Timothy's and Jessie's Mums didn't need the pens for themselves they gave them to Joe and Timothy and Jessie to play with. (Jessie's brother Rupert who went to school wanted his Mum's pens too, and he made a fuss because they had been given to Jessie, but kind Miss Smithers gave her pens to Rupert because when she got them, she found that she didn't really need them.)

Anyway, each of the three friends had a box of coloured pens.

Now, as soon as Joe and Timothy got their Special Offer pens they tried them out at once to see what they wrote like.

Joe tried his pens out on the bottom of his Dad's newspaper because he knew Timothy had got into trouble trying *his* pens out on the gas bill, and of course, as soon as they had tried them out and seen how pretty they were they wanted to begin drawing with them.

Jessie's brother Rupert tried his pens out too, and Jessie watched him. Rupert used his pens to colour some black and white pictures in a comic. Jessie watched Rupert using his Special Offer pens, but she didn't try out her pens at all.

When Joe's Mum went down to pay for the papers, she bought Joe a big drawing-book with white pages to use his pens on; and Timothy's father gave him some wallpaper that had been left over when he had papered the bedroom, and the two little boys had a lovely time drawing things with their Special Offer pens.

Joe drew little tiny pictures in his big drawing-book. He drew little tiny trains, and cars and lorries and tractors, and tiny-tiny people. He sat at the table in his upstairs home among the chimney-pots and drew and drew, very, very slowly. He drew such tiny pictures that there were lots of pictures on each page of his book. All the time he was drawing he popped his tongue in and out.

When Joe's father saw Joe's drawings he said, 'Well, well! I used to draw like that when I was little,' and Joe's Mum said, 'Yes, and you still pop your tongue in and out when you are concentrating hard.' And they both laughed.

Timothy unrolled a lot of wallpaper on to his

bedroom floor to make his drawing. Timothy doesn't draw little pictures like Joe's. He draws big pictures, and the picture he drew with his Special Offer pens was enormous.

Timothy drew a big, long picture. He drew a picture of the Park. He drew trees with green and brown pens and fountains with mauve and blue pens, and people playing tennis and pushing prams and sitting on seats and children swinging on swings with all the pens, one after the other. He drew the Special Lady in her yellow dress with the green dots on it. He drew Joe in his red trousers and Jessie with yellow bows on her hair. He drew the Park keeper and all the flowers. He drew birds eating crumbs and ducks eating crusts, and all the time Timothy drew he talked to himself. He said things like, 'There, Special Lady! That's you running because you are late!' And, 'That's you done, Duck. Now here is a brown crust for you!'

Sometimes Timothy stopped drawing and went off to play 'peep-bo' with Dawn Gloria, his tiny baby sister, and make her laugh. Sometimes he went out to the back yard to say 'hello' to Alfie the cat, but afterwards he always went back and drew a bit more of his Park Picture. *His* Mum said, 'One of these days you'll be a real artist if you go on like that!'

When Timothy couldn't get anything more on to his picture he asked his Mum to roll it up for him so that he could take it upstairs to show his friend Joe.

He carried his rolled-up picture very carefully all the way upstairs, and when he got to the landing where Jessie lived and saw her sitting outside her door playing with her dollie he said, 'I'm going to show Joe my picture, Jessie. Would you like to see it too?'

Jessie said she would like to see it very much and Timothy said, 'There's lots of room for it here. You unroll it for me, Jessie, while I go and fetch Joe.'

So while Timothy went up to fetch Joe, Jessie un-rolled the wallpaper picture, and when Joe and Timothy came down again she had laid it out flat on the landing, and to stop it curling up she had put her dollie on one end of it, and her little toy shopping basket on the other end. Jessie is a very sensible child.

Joe had brought his drawing-book down to show Timothy and Jessie his pictures. They had a lovely time.

Joe and Jessie thought Timothy's Park Picture was very nice. They were pleased to see themselves in it and they recognized the Special Lady at once. 'You are a clever boy, Timothy,' Jessie said.

Then Jessie and Timothy looked at Joe's book, at all the tiny tidy pictures. They thought they were very interesting. Jessie said Joe was a clever boy too. She said, 'You can see which are engines and which are cars, Joe. I think that it is very good.'

Then Timothy said, 'But haven't you drawn anything with your pens, Jessie?' and Jessie said, 'No, not yet'.

Joe said, 'Haven't you any paper? I'll tear the middle out of my drawing book for you if you like.'

And Timothy said, 'I've got lots more wallpaper downstairs, Jessie. You can have some of that.'

But Jessie said that they had plenty of paper in her home. She said her brother Rupert had drawn lots of things with his pens. He had drawn people and cars and trees and animals too. Jessie said, 'I am going to draw something one day. I am going to draw something no one else has done.'

And so she did. For one day, when her brothers Rupert and Philip came home from school they were sucking some very big round sweets. I expect you know the sort of sweets I mean. When you suck them hard they get smaller, and as they get smaller they change colour. Sometimes they are yellow, sometimes brown, sometimes green and sometimes red and sometimes blue and sometimes mauve. Jessie's brothers kept taking them out of their mouths to see what colour they had changed to. They did this until their mother saw them and told them they were to throw them away at once.

Well now, Jessie went away into a corner. She took a piece of paper and she opened her box of Special Offer pens.

First she drew a black circle. 'That's the outside,' she said.

Then inside the black circle she drew a red circle, and inside that an orange circle, and inside the orange circle she drew a yellow circle, and inside the yellow circle she drew a green circle, and inside the green circle she drew a blue one and inside the blue one she made a mauve one, and there was just room to fill in the very middle with a big brown dot.

'Look everybody,' Jessie said, 'I've drawn a gob-stopper!' And she ran outside and went to look for Joe and Timothy to show them her picture.

'Remember, remember —'

There was a time when the Park where Joe and his friends Timothy and Jessie used to play began to look very cold and bare. All the bright coloured flowers in the flower-beds had died and their dry bare stems had been tidied away.

The goldfish who lived in the fountains hid themselves among the dark lily-roots, and the leaves fell off the trees and were swept up by the park keepers who made them into heaps and burned them.

The Special Lady who plays games with the children who come to the Park said, 'Look at the blue smoke going up to the sky.'

She said, 'It reminds me that it will soon be November the Fifth.'

The Special Lady said that when she was a little girl her father used to save up all the leaves from his apple-trees and all the rubbish from his garden to make a Fifth of November bonfire.

When she said this all the children began to talk about

November the Fifth and fireworks and bonfires – they got so excited that some of them shouted and the Special Lady had to shout louder than them to be heard.

'Quiet, quiet,' she shouted. And when they were all quiet again she told them about being careful and not being silly and doing showing-off things on Bonfire Night, and when they'd all listened and said that *they* wouldn't be silly, she taught them a funny old song that said,

'Remember, remember the Fifth of November,
The gunpowder treason and plot.
I see no reason why gunpowder treason
Should ever be forgot.'

And she made up a good jumping, running, arms-up-and-downing game to do while they sang it, and they jumped and ran about until they were as warm as little bonfires themselves.

After that and right up until November the Fifth came, Joe, Timothy and Jessie did nothing but talk about it. When they went shopping with their mothers and saw the fireworks in the glass cases under the shop counters they were very excited. They talked and talked about the splendid bonfire *they* would have.

'And we'll be very careful and not show off,' said Joe.

Then Jessie remembered something. She said, 'Joe and I haven't got anywhere to make a bonfire, Timothy; we shall have to come to yours. You will have to have it in your yard.'

But oh dear! When you live in a tall, tall house with only a small backyard with rabbit hutches and coal-bins in it and people's windows looking down on it you can't have bonfires. You can't have even a very little one.

Timothy's Mum said so. She said, 'Really, you children do get funny ideas. We'd never be allowed to do such a thing, and even if we were, I shouldn't want all the smoke and blacks blowing into my windows.'

When Timothy's mother said this, Timothy saw that of course, there would never have been room for a bonfire, *and* the hutches, *and* the coal-bins, and he was very very sad.

Joe was very sad too, because Timothy went straight upstairs to tell him at once. 'Oh dear,' he said, 'I *did* want us to have a bonfire.'

Joe's Mum said, 'Never mind. It can't be helped.'

But Joe said, '*Everyone* will have bonfires but us.'

And when he said '*Everyone*' like that his Mum started to laugh.

' Why, of *course* !' she said. 'Of course you will have a bonfire. You will have lots and lots of bonfires AND fireworks ! Don't worry – just wait and see.' And she laughed again. She wouldn't say anything more then, but when Joe was in bed that night he heard her laughing and talking to his Dad, and then he heard his Dad laughing too! It was very mysterious.

The next day Joe's Mum talked to Jessie's and Timothy's mothers and they laughed too. But although the children wondered and asked lots of questions their mothers only said, 'You'll have more bonfires than you can count.'

And that's all they would say.

When the Fifth of November came the big house seemed full of smiles and secrets, but the children still couldn't think how they were going to have lots of bonfires. There was no sign of a bonfire being built in the backyard, and no one had collected any piles of rubbish to burn.

The day went by and evening came. Joe had finished his tea and was sitting looking at a story-book when there was a 'rattle-rattle-rattle' at the letter-box. When Joe's Dad opened the door – there stood Jessie!

Jessie was wearing her outdoor coat and her pink woollen bonnet and her furry boots. Joe was surprised to see her dressed like that. Jessie was looking surprised too. 'My Mum told me to come up,' she said.

And there was Timothy coming up the stairs! He had his coat on too – it had a hood on it, and the hood was buttoned under his chin and his Dad's big green scarf was wrapped round him and tied in a big knot behind his back.

'Now for those bonfires,' said Joe's Dad.

And while his Dad helped him into his coat, his Mum fastened on his old red cap with the ear-flaps, and helped him on with his outdoor shoes. Then she and Joe's Dad put their coats on.

'Come on, into your coat, Joey,' said Joe's father.

But they *didn't go downstairs*. The children went towards the door but Joe's Dad said, 'No, this way!'

So they went, following Joe's Mum and Joe's Dad. Out of the living-room, into the kitchen and out of the kitchen window on to the roof among the chimney-pots!

And what do you think Joe's kind Mum had thought of, and his kind Dad had made? It was a strong wooden platform, up against the brick wall, high enough for the children to stand on and see over the top.

Joe's Dad lifted them up, one at a time.

'There!' said Joe's Mum. 'There they are! You've got all the bonfires for miles around.'

And there, far below they could see bonfires in all the yards and gardens of the town – hundreds of them! And Joe, Timothy and Jessie could see them all from the roof of their tall, tall house on the top of the hill.

Some fires were smoky and flickery, some were hot and fierce and sent up thousands of bright sparks; some were like burning rings with darkness in the middle, and some were tall like towers. Now and again a fire turned red, or green or blue, and Joe's Dad told them that that was because someone was putting coloured powder on it. When that happened Jessie said, 'Ooh!'

And everywhere around the bonfires were the twinkling, winking, flashing, dashing reds, blues, greens and yellows of fireworks. Rockets rushed up into the air from this place and that and burst into brightness all over the sky.

'Oh,' said Jessie. 'Oh. I just love those rockets with the coloured lights. They look so floating and pretty.'

'I like the gold and silver twinkly ones best,' said Joe.

But Timothy said he liked golden whirly-whirly screaming ones because they made him think of the time his cat Alfie had a fight with Mrs Lambert's cat Fluffy.

'Look,' they kept shouting. 'Look, look, look!'

And somehow there were other people on the rooftop, shouting and pointing. There was Jessie's mother who had bought a bag of toffees for everyone to suck. Jessie's Dad had taken the big children to a special bonfire on a field behind the bus garage. Joe's Dad pointed out where it was, and although they knew it was a very big bonfire indeed it was so far away that it looked quite tiny.

Timothy's Dad had come with some hot potatoes that Timothy's Mum had baked in her oven. She couldn't come because she had to mind their baby, Dawn Gloria, and Alfie their cat who didn't like bonfire nights.

Joe's Mum had made hot soup for everyone and Jessie's mother lifted the mugs through the window for her.

Everyone had a lovely warm meal of hot potatoes and soup out there on the rooftop.

Then, when they had finished their supper Timothy's Dad said he had a surprise for them. He had brought some of those safe sparkling white fireworks with wire handles.

'Two each for everyone,' he said, and while he went into Joe's Dad's rooftop greenhouse to light them, Joe's father brought out his tomato-watering bucket full of water.

'I know they're safe fireworks,' he said, 'but we don't want to upset that Special Lady of yours, do we? So, when they have burned out, kindly drop them in the bucket.'

Joe, Timothy and Jessie stood up on their platform, high above the town, and waved their sparklers up and down and round and round, making pretty patterns in the air. Some of the people down below looked up and wondered about these pretty waving lights. But the children didn't know that. They were singing:

'Remember, remember the Fifth of November
The gunpowder treason and plot.
I see no reason why gunpowder treason
Should ever be forgot.'

They sang and waved and waved and sang until their sparklers burned out into little red fire-worms that sizzled

out when they dropped them into the tomato-watering bucket.

'There,' said Joe's Mum a little while later, when she tucked him up in his warm bed with his teddy-bear hot-water bottle to keep him cosy. 'I said you'd have a lot of bonfires, didn't I?'

And Joe said, 'I'll have them next year too, won't I?' And shut his eyes, and saw all the dancing lights again in his thoughts until he went to sleep.

Going away

Jessie the little brown girl has a pretty grown-up cousin called Rosa who used to work in a hairdresser's shop in the middle of the big smoky town.

Everybody in Jessie's family loved Cousin Rosa – she was always so happy and kind. She used to come over to the tall house on her day off and cut and set the hair of some of the ladies who lived there.

You could always tell when Cousin Rosa was having a day off, because there would be ladies with hairnets on talking to each other on the landings and drinking cups of tea, and everyone would be laughing and joking because Jessie's grown-up cousin had been telling them funny stories while she did their hair.

Cousin Rosa worked late at the shop and did the tall house ladies' hair for them on her day off because she was saving up her money to go back home to Jamaica and open her own hairdressing shop and marry the steady boyfriend who was waiting for her there!

One day, when Joe was on his way downstairs to look

for Timothy, he found Jessie sitting on the landing out-side her door crying and crying. Joe had never seen any-one crying such big fat tears before. He stared very hard when the large wet drops fell on to the landing floor. In fact, he was so interested he almost forgot to ask poor Jessie what she was crying *for*. But he didn't quite forget!

'Oh, oh dear,' Jessie said, shaking her head so that all her bright red ribbons jumped and bumped. 'My Cousin Rosa has looked into her Savings Book and she says she's got enough money at last. She's going to take a plane and go back home to Jamaica and we're all very, very sad.'

Joe felt very sorry for Jessie when he heard this, so he sat down on the floor next to her and patted her back.

'My Auntie Grace is going to make a fine party for her on Saturday,' Jessie said, 'and everyone is going to sing and dance and give her wedding-presents.' And then she cried again.

Just then Jessie's Mum came out to fetch her to have her face washed and Joe saw that she had been crying too. This made him feel so sad his own eyes felt quite wet, and when he told Timothy about Rosa's going-away and about Jessie crying his voice sounded quite sad too.

But Timothy's mother who had been listening said, 'She'll soon cheer up. After all, Jessie's Mum says they'll all be going back home for a holiday one day, so they'll see Rosa again. Look what a good time they'll have when they meet in Jamaica.'

So, all the ladies in the tall house who were Rosa's customers collected money and Mr Lemon went to the wholesaler's and bought her a lovely dinner-service in a red-and-white striped box to take home with her, and a new person came to live in Rosa's little room in Auntie Grace's house.

It wasn't long before Jessie was saying, 'We've had a letter from Rosa. She says she had a *smashing* wedding. When I grow up I can go and spend a holiday with her,

I can stay in her new bungalow. She says it's all among the banana-trees! I shall like that!'

And she jumped and played and laughed again and wasn't sad any more – just as Timothy's Mum had said.

Now there was a very old man who lived in the tall, tall house. He was called Mr Gardiner and he had a little room right at the end of the passage. He was Mrs Lemon's old father and every day she took him breakfast and dinner and tea because he was too old to cook for himself.

Mr Gardiner couldn't walk very far, but sometimes he would come out of his room and sit in an armchair by his landing window. He liked to look out at the rooftops and throw crumbs to the birds.

Now and again, when Joe and Timothy and Jessie wanted something to do, they would go along and say 'Hello' to him.

Sometimes he would say 'Hello' back, but sometimes he would close his eyes and pretend to be asleep and they would walk quietly away again.

The children liked Mr Gardiner because he looked such a kind old man. He had a white fluffy beard like Father Christmas and a grey woollen cap that he could pull over his ears if he felt cold.

One day though, Joe's Mum said to him, 'Joe – a very sad thing has happened. Poor old Mr Gardiner has died. Poor old man.'

So for the next day or two the children in the tall house were very good and quiet. Joe's Mum went all round the house collecting money from people to buy a funeral wreath, and Joe went with her. When they got to Timothy's home, which was right at the bottom, she stopped and had a cup of tea with Timothy's mother, and the two little boys whispered together.

'What's a wreath?' said Timothy.

'I don't know,' said Joe. 'It's something to do with dying.'

'I don't like dying very much,' Timothy said. 'It's too whispery and sad.'

The next morning all the people who lived in the front of the tall house, pulled their window curtains together, and Joe's Mum and Timothy's Mum told them it was because today was to be Mr Gardiner's funeral day. Joe's Mum and Timothy's Mum were so sad when they said this, that both the little boys decided to go to look for each other at the same time, and they met as they often did on Jessie's landing. . .

'My Mum made Mrs Lemon a cake and Mrs Lambert cooked her a ham,' whispered Joe. 'I think, a funeral is a sort of sad party like they had when Jessie's Cousin Rosa went to Jamaica.'

'My Mum said old Mr Gardiner had *gone home*, Joe!' Timothy whispered back. 'Just like Rosa did!'

As they were near Jessie's home they thought they'd

go and talk to her and see what she thought about dying, so they went quietly across the landing and rattled softly at the letter box of the door of her home.

Jessie's Mum opened it at once.

'Come in, children,' she said in a very soft voice. 'You don't want to be outside just this minute because they've brought the funeral carriage round. Mrs Lemon wanted her father driven off from his own home.'

Jessie's Mum had pulled the yellow curtains in her sitting-room window, so the room was full of yellow light, but she had left a tiny slit at the side, and they were able to look down on the street by the front door of the tall house.

There was a big black motor outside, with piles of flowers on the roof.

'Is it a sort of wedding?' said Jessie.

Then Joe remembered something. 'When I was at my Country Gran's once I saw a car like that near the Church there. There were lots of flowers, I remember, and people crying and some men were putting a big box into the ground. Country Gran said the people had sent the flowers.'

'They are wreaths,' whispered Jessie's mother. 'Like your Mum collected for and we all sent, Joe.'

The children looked hard at the wreaths on top of the black car.

'People collected for wedding presents when Rosa

went home,' said Jessie. 'You have flowers at weddings, too.'

Just then some people began to come out of the front of the tall house, and another black car drove up behind the one with flowers on.

'Come away now, children,' said Jessie's Mum. 'This bit has nothing to do with us,' and she pulled the curtain right across at the side.

'I don't think dying is like going home to be married though,' said Joe.

'I saw a dead cat once,' said Timothy. 'It was near those trees with the white flowers on, in the Park. It was very, very still. My Dad said it had gone to sleep for ever and ever.'

'Oh dear,' said Jessie, 'I wish everyone wasn't so sad!'

'Never mind,' Timothy told her. 'You cried and cried when Rosa went, but you soon cheered up. You'll see her again when you go to visit her in her banana-tree bungalow.'

Jessie's Mum had been washing up the tea things, but just then she came into the room, so she said, 'We will *all* see that old Mr Gardiner someday when we get to that happy, happy place where he has gone.'

Then she said, 'Well, you little boys, it's all over, so, if you want to go back home to your Mummies it will be quite all right,' and she pulled back the window curtains so that the ordinary white sunlight could come in again.

Joe went upstairs to his cosy home among the chimney-pots to tell his mother all the things they had seen and talked about.

'Jessie's Mum says dying is going to a happy, happy place,' he told his Mum.

And she said, 'Let's hope she's right at that.'

Joe's Mum's birthday party

Lots of people in the tall house where Joe and Timothy live have special treats on their birthdays.

Joe had his birthday on one of the days when they went to the Park to play games with the Special Lady, so all the children sang 'Happy Birthday' to him, and the Special Lady gave everyone three sweets from her Birthday Tin. Afterwards his Mum asked Jessie and Timothy upstairs to tea with them, and they had shrimps and a chocolate cake with 'Joe' written on it in yellow icing flowers, that his Country Gran had made for him.

On Jessie's birthday she went with her Dad and her Mum and her brothers and sisters to visit a Zoo in the country. They had ice-creams in a café near the monkey's cage, and the monkey made faces at Jessie's brother George and he made faces back. Jessie said it was lovely.

Timothy's birthday was on a Sunday, when his Dad was home, so he went with his Dad and Mum and the baby to see Timothy's Uncle Reggie and Auntie Joy who live by the river, and Uncle Reggie took Timothy and his Dad out for a row in his boat. That was lovely too.

But no one in the tall, tall house ever had a birthday like the one Joe's Mum had. It was so special that the people there will never stop talking about it.

Now, Joe's mother is a very kind, smiling, singing sort of lady and everyone likes her. She is always doing things for people and cheering them up when they are miserable.

One day Joe came hurrying downstairs from his high-up home and found Jessie and Timothy waiting on the landing outside Jessie's door. Jessie's mother had given them an orange each and one for Joe. They had put Joe's orange on the floor but had started to eat theirs, and as Joe came down he smelt the orangey smell and when he got to the landing Timothy and Jessie were already very sticky. But Joe was so excited he didn't bother about the smell or the stickiness.

Joe hardly noticed what Jessie and Timothy were doing, and certainly didn't notice the orange on the floor that was his! In fact, he was in such a hurry to talk to his friends that he kicked it by mistake and it went bumpetty-bumpetty down to the underneath landing before anyone could stop it.

Of course, they ran down after it; but when they had found it and Joe had started to peel it straight away he remembered his news all over again.

He said, 'My Daddy says that my Mum is going to

have a birthday very soon. He says it's the most impor-
tant birthday you can have. He is going to take some time
off tomorrow and he's going to take me out with him to
buy her a really special birthday present.'

Now Joe and Timothy and Jessie were so busy with
their talk and their oranges that they didn't see a rather
cross old lady called Mrs Gravey coming up the stairs. If
Joe had seen her he wouldn't have shouted so loudly,
but because he was excited he shouted, 'My Dad says

Mum will have the Key of the Door! He is going to buy her a birthday card with red roses and a big key on it!'

But Mrs Gravey didn't grumble at Joe for making so much noise. She was quite interested. When she took out the key of *her* door from her handbag she said, 'Is that your mammy then, Joe?' and Joe said, 'Yes.'

And Mrs Gravey said, 'Well, well, fancy that now! H'm, h'm. Twenty-one, eh? A nice young person your mammy is, Joe. Looked after me when I wasn't well that time. H'm, h'm.'

And she went indoors to her home without grumbling at the children for making a noise or asking them not to leave any orange-peel about.

They wouldn't have left any peel about anyway, but Mrs Gravey usually said things like that.

Now Mrs Gravey is a lady who likes to talk and talk, and so she talked to everyone about Joe's Mum's birthday. She told Mrs Lambert who lives under Joe's home, and Mrs Lambert said, 'We must do something about that! That young woman has been very good about keeping quiet while my Arnie has been on nights.'

Mrs Lemon whose husband drives a big lorry said, 'Yes, and she often does a bit of shopping for me when my legs are bad.'

And all the other people in the big house remembered nice things about Joe's Mum; about her minding their

77

cats and feeding their birds and altering their dresses for them, and everyone said, 'Something must be done about Joe's mother's Twenty-First Birthday.'

And they all began to think, and whisper together and make plans and be very, very secret.

And this is what happened!

On the night before Joe's mother's birthday when most of the tall house people were asleep, Mr Lemon and Jessie's Dad crept upstairs and stood a big board against the wall opposite Joe's front door.

On top of the board Mr Lemon had painted 'Congratulations and Many Happy Returns' in lovely curly writing, and pinned all over the board were birthday cards from every family in the big house – special twenty-first birthday cards with silver and gold keys and white ribbon on them. Wasn't that a wonderful surprise?

Joe's mother thought so the next morning when she opened her door to fetch in the milk.

Although she wasn't dressed she had Joe's present, which was a blue and yellow silky scarf, tied over her dressing-gown, and Joe's Daddy's present which was a pair of sparkly ear-rings in her ears and she was humming a song to herself, but, when she saw the big board and the birthday cards she said 'Oh!' right out loud.

And as soon as she said that, Arnie Lambert who had been listening downstairs began to sing 'Happy Birthday' and all the other people in the tall house who had been listening with their doors open joined in and sang too. Wasn't *that* lovely?

But even *that* wasn't all!

For while Mr Lemon had been painting the birthday-card board Timothy's Dad had been helping to hang up flags in the downstairs hall, and that night the people in the tall, tall house gave a party there. They put chairs all round the hall and the families who lived down there opened their doors so that people could go in and out and boil kettles on their gas-stoves and wash up in their sinks.

When Joe's Mum went downstairs to her party she said 'OH' again. For there on a table in the middle of the hall was a grand birthday cake with a golden '21' on it, and there were lots of lovely things to eat and drink, and everyone was smiling.

Jessie's brothers had brought over their record-player and people danced on the landings, and Mrs Gravey brought out a big box full of funny hats – it was just like Christmas.

Then Mr Lemon said, 'Quiet, everyone. It's time to cut the cake,' and Joe's Mum had to go and put a knife into her lovely birthday cake.

Everyone said, 'Speech, speech. Say something.' But Joe's mother just shook her head, and laughed.

Then Joe had a good idea, he said, 'Mum, sing that song

you sang to Daddy and me this morning,' and his father said, 'Yes, that's it.'

So instead of making a speech she sang:

'I'm twenty-one today. I've got the key of the door.
 I've never been twenty-one before. So shout hip-hip-
   hooray!
 Now I can do as I like – I'm twenty-one today!'

And everyone laughed and joined in.

And, although it was late before anyone went to bed that night, Joe, Timothy and Jessie stayed up to the very end!